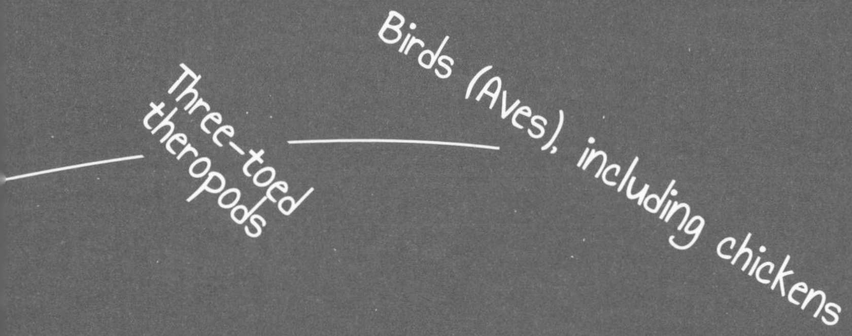
Birds (Aves), including chickens
Three-toed theropods

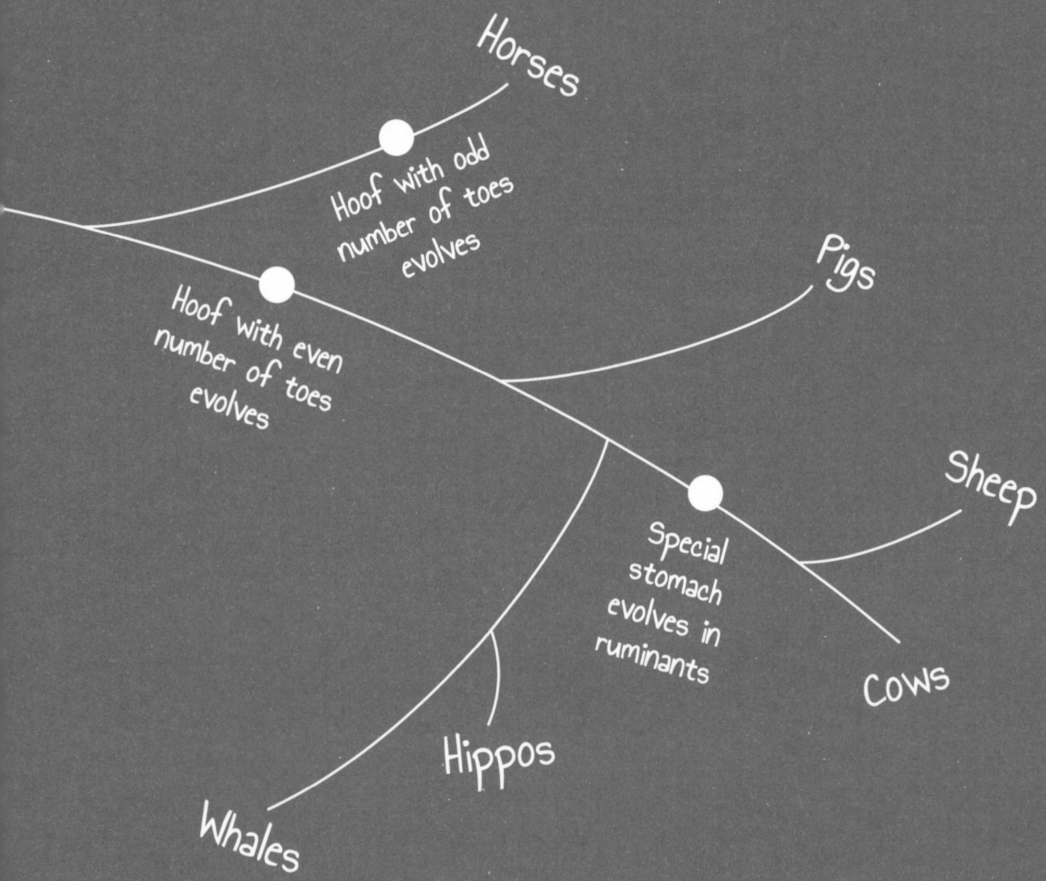
Horses
Hoof with odd number of toes evolves
Pigs
Hoof with even number of toes evolves
Sheep
Special stomach evolves in ruminants
Cows
Hippos
Whales

Chicken Frank, DINOSAUR!

S. K. Wenger
illustrated by Jojo Ensslin

Albert Whitman & Company
Chicago, Illinois

For Keira—who follows her roar and leads with her heart—SKW

To Martha and Robert, world's greatest paleontologists—JE

Library of Congress Cataloging-in-Publication data is on file with the publisher.
Text copyright © 2021 by S. K. Wenger
Illustrations copyright © 2021 by Albert Whitman & Company
Illustrations by Jojo Ensslin
First published in the United States of America in 2021 by Albert Whitman & Company
ISBN 978-0-8075-1141-1 (hardcover)
ISBN 978-0-8075-1142-8 (ebook)
Printed in China
10 9 8 7 6 5 4 3 2 1 WKT 26 25 24 23 22 21

Design by Rick DeMonico

For more information about Albert Whitman & Company,
visit our website at www.albertwhitman.com.

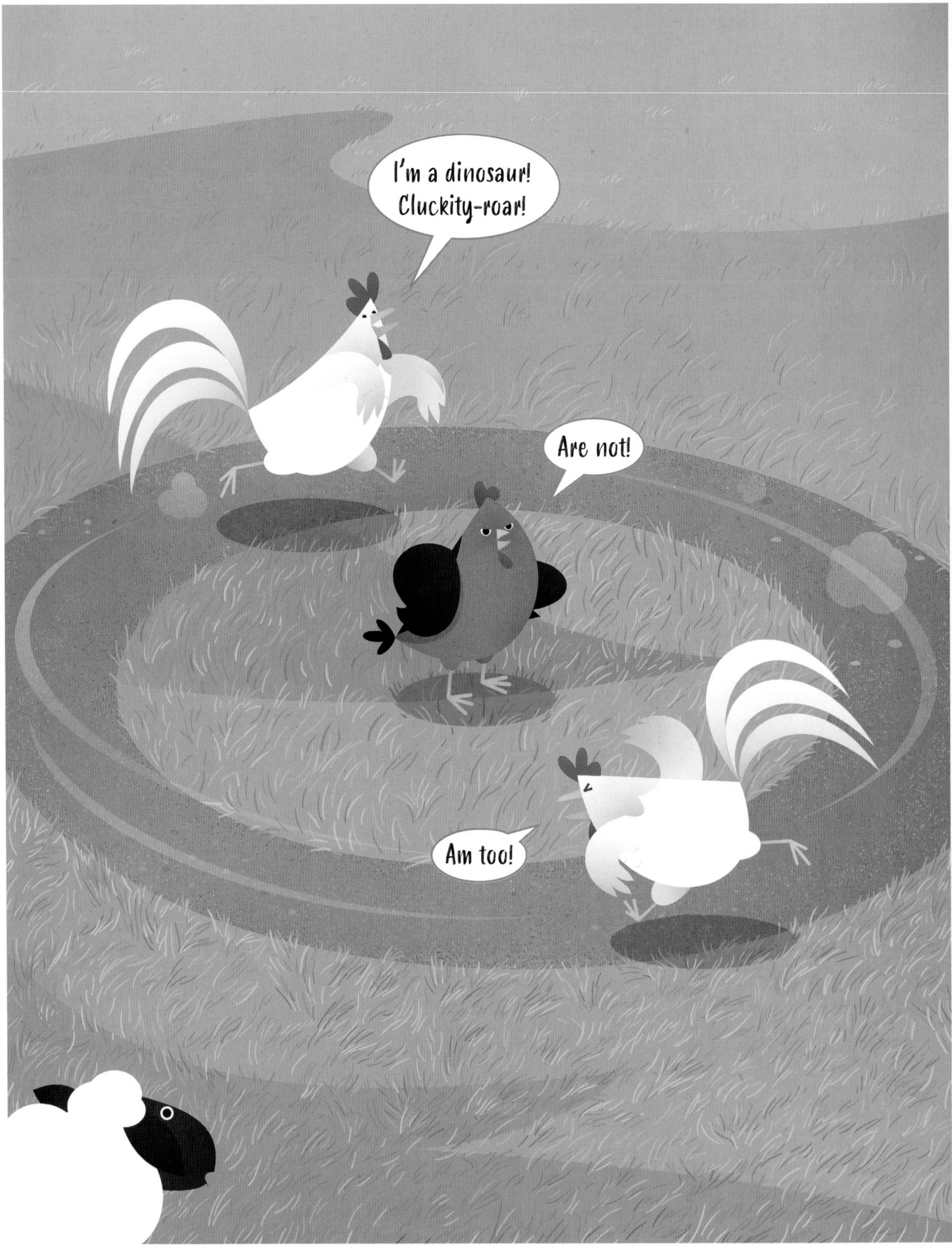
I'm a dinosaur!
Cluckity-roar!
Are not!
Am too!

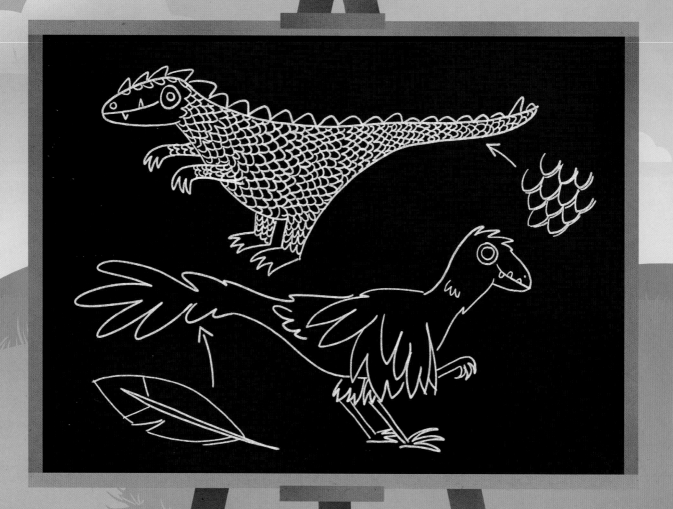

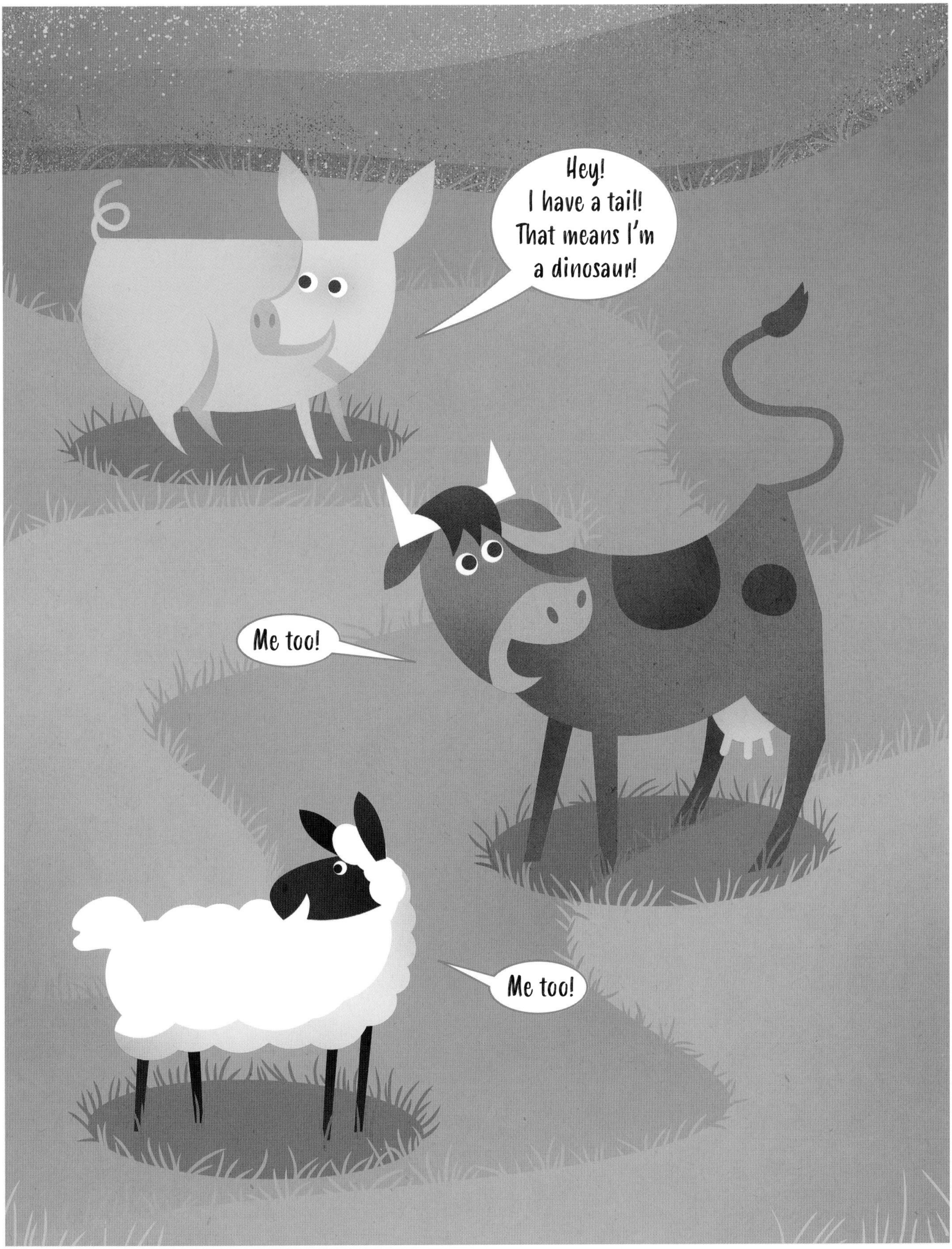
Hey! I have a tail! That means I'm a dinosaur!
Me too!
Me too!

No, no, no! I'm a reptile.
You're mammals with fur—
Reptiles
Amphibians
Birds
Mammals
Fish
You call this fur?

Dear Ike,
    We share a
common ancestor!
Let's have a
    reunion!
Your cousin,
        Frank

TO:

Ike Alligator
Swamp,
    Louisiana

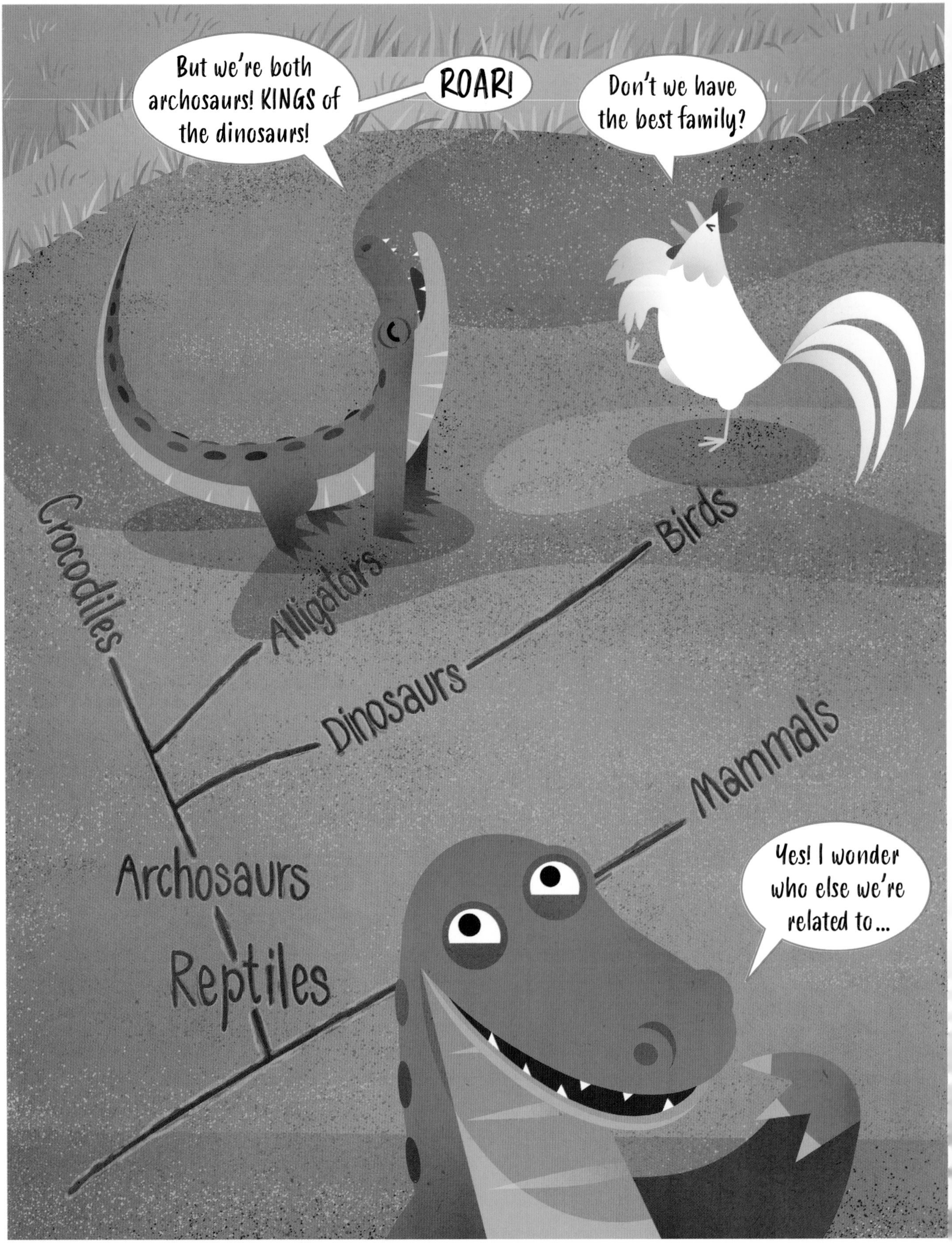
But we're both archosaurs! KINGS of the dinosaurs!
ROAR!
Don't we have the best family?
Crocodiles
Alligators
Birds
Dinosaurs
Mammals
Archosaurs
Reptiles
Yes! I wonder who else we're related to...

Later, at the aquarium
Wait! This one has a horn!
A swimming unicorn!
Even better.

What Is DNA?

DNA is an abbreviation for a big word: **d**eoxyribo**n**ucleic **a**cid.

DNA is a molecule that holds your genes.

Your genes came from your parents and determine your traits—from the color of your hair, eyes, and skin to how tall you will grow to whether you can roll your tongue. DNA is found in every cell of your body. It carries the code for how you are made, just as it does for every other organism on the planet.

Changes to the code of DNA can happen. These changes are called mutations, and they can create variations in a trait, like stunted tails or missing teeth. Over time, these mutations can become more common, especially if they are useful, like longer snouts in anteaters and beaks of different sizes in birds.

What Is Evolution?

Evolution happens to populations of living things over time. In order for evolution to occur, variation in traits needs to exist. Different colors of fur is an example of variation. If one form of a trait helps a population survive better, it can become more common over time.

Peppered moths live in the United States and the United Kingdom, and two forms of wing color occur—light and dark. Before the 1900s, the lighter speckled pattern was more common. It blended in with grayish bark on trees. Blending in with their environment helped peppered moths hide from birds looking for tasty moths to eat.

When tree trunks became dark with soot from industry and manufacturing, the light-colored moths stood out, making them easy pickings for birds. Over time, the color of peppered moths shifted as darker moths survived longer and reproduced.

Later, air became cleaner, tree trunks became lighter, and the color of moths shifted back.

Is Chicken Frank Really Related to *T. rex*?

Because dinosaurs existed so long ago, you might think it would be hard to tell. But scientific evidence in fossils and molecular testing on tissues show that YES they are related. The path for this discovery began with a bone from a *T. rex* that had to be cut in half before it could be airlifted from its dig site in Montana by helicopter. Studies on the bone's interior revealed soft tissue. Tests on the tissue indicate *T. rex* has more in common with chickens and ostriches than it has in common with alligators and lizards. Comparisons in the fossil record show physical similarities, including hip shape and the presence of wishbones.

Similarities Between Dinosaurs, Chickens, and Alligators

EGGS!

Dinosaurs laid eggs, just like birds, alligators, and other reptiles do. Fossils of eggs have been found with baby dinosaurs inside. Dinosaur eggs, like those of birds, had hard shells made of calcium. Calcium is a mineral that helps make your bones strong. It also helps protect the embryo inside the egg and prevent water loss so the egg doesn't dry out. Alligator eggs start out hard but become leathery as the baby alligator grows inside.

FEET!

It's easy to see the similarities in bone structure between a chicken and a *T. rex*. However, a chicken can do one thing that *T. rex* couldn't do: perch. A slight change in position of the bones connected to the rear toe and an increase in their length allowed for this gripping action.

TAILS!

Chickens have reptilian-looking tails during early stages of growth in the egg. The tail becomes shorter, as some bones fuse and others disappear before hatching. The changes to the tail are due to changes in DNA that occurred over time.

TEETH!

Scientists studying evolution found that under the right conditions, tiny teeth can form on the beak of a chicken before it hatches. These teeth are an example of a trait that is no longer commonly made by DNA. But they used to be! A flying, feathered dinosaur called *Archeopteryx* had teeth.

THE EGG TOOTH!

Although modern chickens don't have teeth, they do have one "tooth" that is very important: the egg tooth! Both alligators and chicks have an egg tooth for cracking themselves out of their shells. On the chick, it is found at the end of the upper beak. On the alligator, it is found at the end of the nose. The egg tooth falls off after the animal hatches.

SCALES OR FEATHERS?

Do reptiles have scales or feathers? Birds are reptiles. Dinosaurs are reptiles. So reptiles can have both! In fact, birds have scales and feathers, because they have scales on their feet. Fossils show that some dinosaurs also had feathers.

But how are reptile scales and bird feathers connected? Feathers come from the same structures in the skin that make scales. The first "feathers" were simple—no more than hollow tubes, which probably helped hold body heat or provide camouflage. Over time, these tubes became thinner, longer, and divided to resemble the feathers we know today.

Frank's Glossary of Favorite Animal Groups

Aves: The group of egg-laying animals with feathers and wings that usually can fly, commonly known as birds. Their eggs have special membranes inside the shell that help to keep the egg from drying out and allow air to flow in and out.

Amphibians: Animals that are rarely found far from water and can move on to land. Their special skin helps them breathe and needs to stay moist to do so. This group includes frogs, toads, salamanders, and newts.

Archosaurs: Egg-laying reptiles with longer back legs and shorter front legs, who diverged into 2 main groups—the crocodilians and the dinosaurs. Archosaurs that still exist today include crocodiles, alligators, and birds (a.k.a. modern dinosaurs).

> **Crocodilians** walk with limbs sprawled out to the sides of their bodies.
> **Dinosaurs** walk with limbs positioned underneath their bodies.

Fishes: Animals with streamlined bodies that swim in fresh and saltwater habitats of the world. Most have fins for swimming and gills for breathing. Lungfish have both lungs and gills.

Lepidosaurs: Reptiles with scaly skin whose modern animals include snakes and lizards.

Mammals: Animals that have fur and lungs for breathing. Offspring are nourished with milk from their mothers.

Reptiles: Animals with scales on their skin and lungs for breathing. Most lay eggs.

Ruminants: A group of animals that includes cows and sheep, who have stomachs made of four chambers. These special stomachs help them get nutrients from the plants that they eat.

Sharks: A group of fish with gills and an internal skeleton made of cartilage.

Theropods: A dinosaur group with some features that are similar to birds, such as hollow bones, three-toed limbs, and bipedal locomotion. Bipedal means they walked on two feet like Chicken Frank!

Frank's Family Tree: The Favorite Parts!

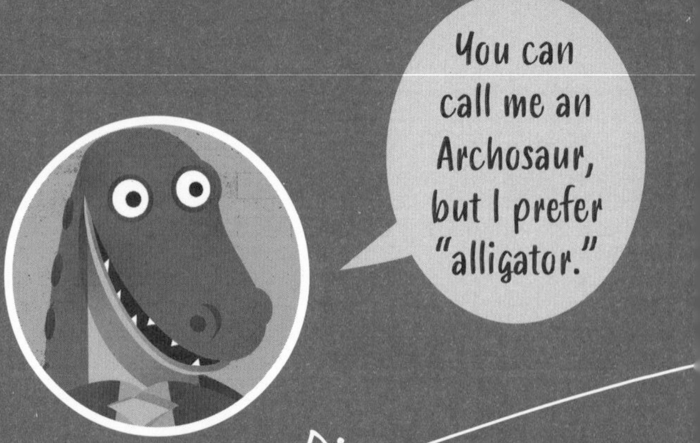

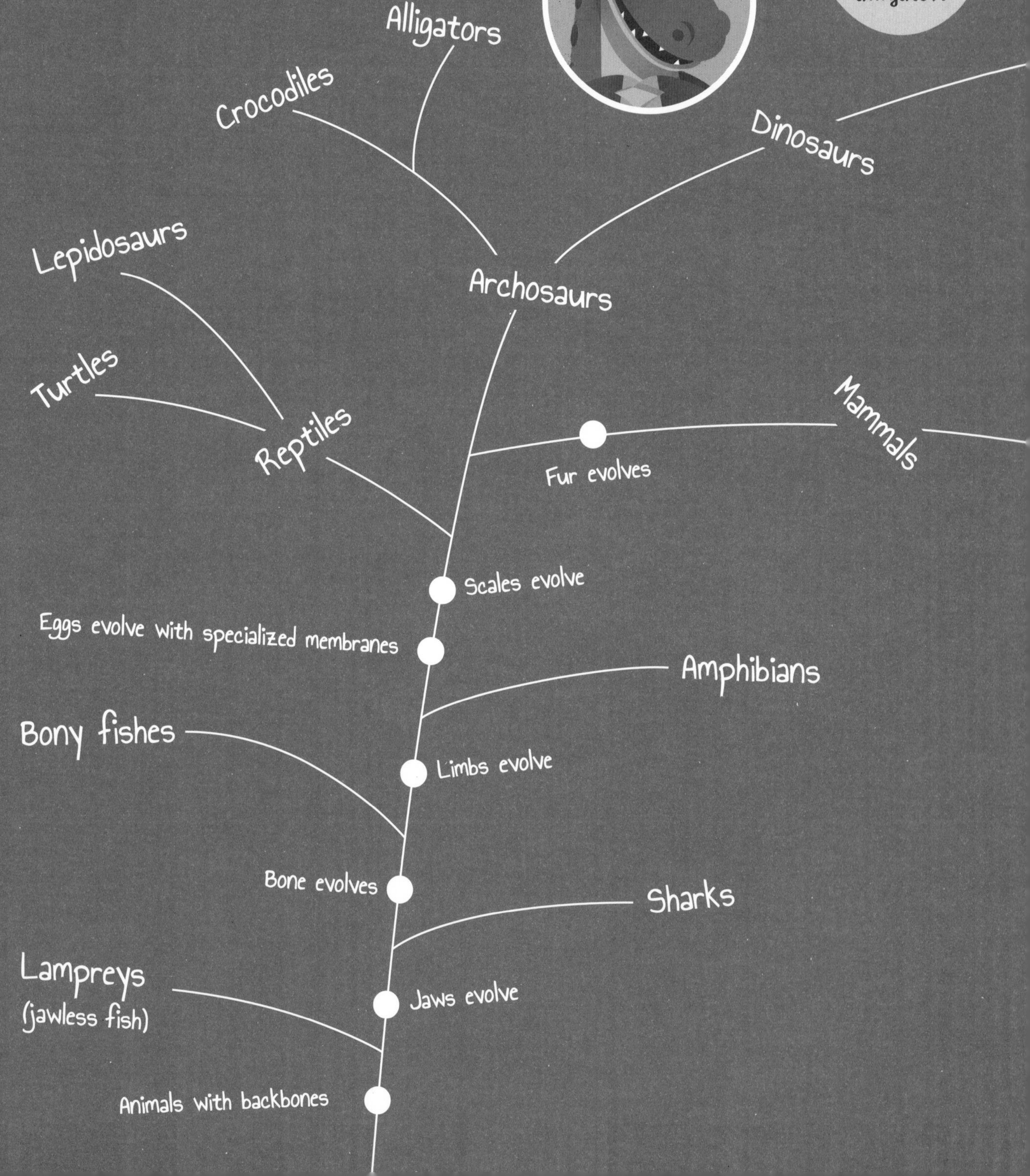